STAR WARS®

THE CLONE WARS™

SLAVES OF THE REPUBLIC
VOLUME ONE
"THE MYSTERY OF KIROS"

SCRIPT
HENRY GILROY

PENCILS
SCOTT HEPBURN

INKS
DAN PARSONS

COLORS
MICHAEL E. WIGGAM

LETTERING
MICHAEL HEISLER

COVER ART
DAVE FILONI

War spreads across the galaxy! From the Inner Core to the Outer Rim, the epic struggle grows as Republic clone troopers under the command of the Jedi Knights battle Count Dooku and the droid armies of the Separatists on the frontlines of a thousand planets. Early in the fight, both factions struggle to win allies, secure resources, and control strategic positions, in hopes of turning the tide in their favor as the scope of the Clone Wars expands.

Even neutral worlds desperately trying to remain at peace are pulled into the fray. Forced to pick sides, they must choose their allies well or take the chance of having their planets turned into a battleground and laid to waste. None know this better than the inhabitants of the Kiros system, where the proud-historied colony of Togruta faces this crucial dilemma . . .

DARK HORSE COMICS

 Spotlight

VISIT US AT
www.abdopublishing.com

Reinforced library bound edition published in 2010 by Spotlight, a division of the ABDO Group, 80 West 78th Street, Edina, Minnesota 55439. Spotlight produces high-quality reinforced library bound editions for schools and libraries. Published by agreement with Dark Horse Comics, Inc., and Lucasfilm Ltd.

Printed in the United States of America, Melrose Park, Illinois.
092009
012010

 PRINTED ON RECYCLED PAPER

Library of Congress Cataloging-in-Publication Data

Gilroy, Henry.
  Slaves of the republic / script by Henry Gilroy ; pencils by Scott
Hepburn ; inks by Dan Parsons ; colors by Michael E. Wiggam ;
lettering by Michael Heisler.
-- Reinforced library bound ed.
     v. cm. -- (Star wars: the clone wars)
  "Dark Horse Comics."
  Contents: v. 1. The mystery of Kiros -- v. 2. Slave traders of Zygerria --
v. 3. The depths of Zygerria -- v. 4. Auction of a million souls -- v. 5. A
slave now, a slave forever -- v. 6. Escape from kadavo.
  ISBN 978-1-59961-710-7 (v. 1) -- ISBN 978-1-59961-711-4 (v. 2) --
ISBN 978-1-59961-712-1 (v. 3) -- ISBN 978-1-59961-713-8 (v. 4) --
ISBN 978-1-59961-714-5 (v. 5) -- ISBN 978-1-59961-715-2 (v. 6)
  1. Graphic novels. [1. Graphic novels.] I. Hepburn, Scott. II. Star
Wars, the clone wars (Television program) III. Title.
  PZ7.7.G55Sl 2010
  [Fic]--dc22
                          2009030553

All Spotlight books have reinforced library bindings and
are manufactured in the United States of America.

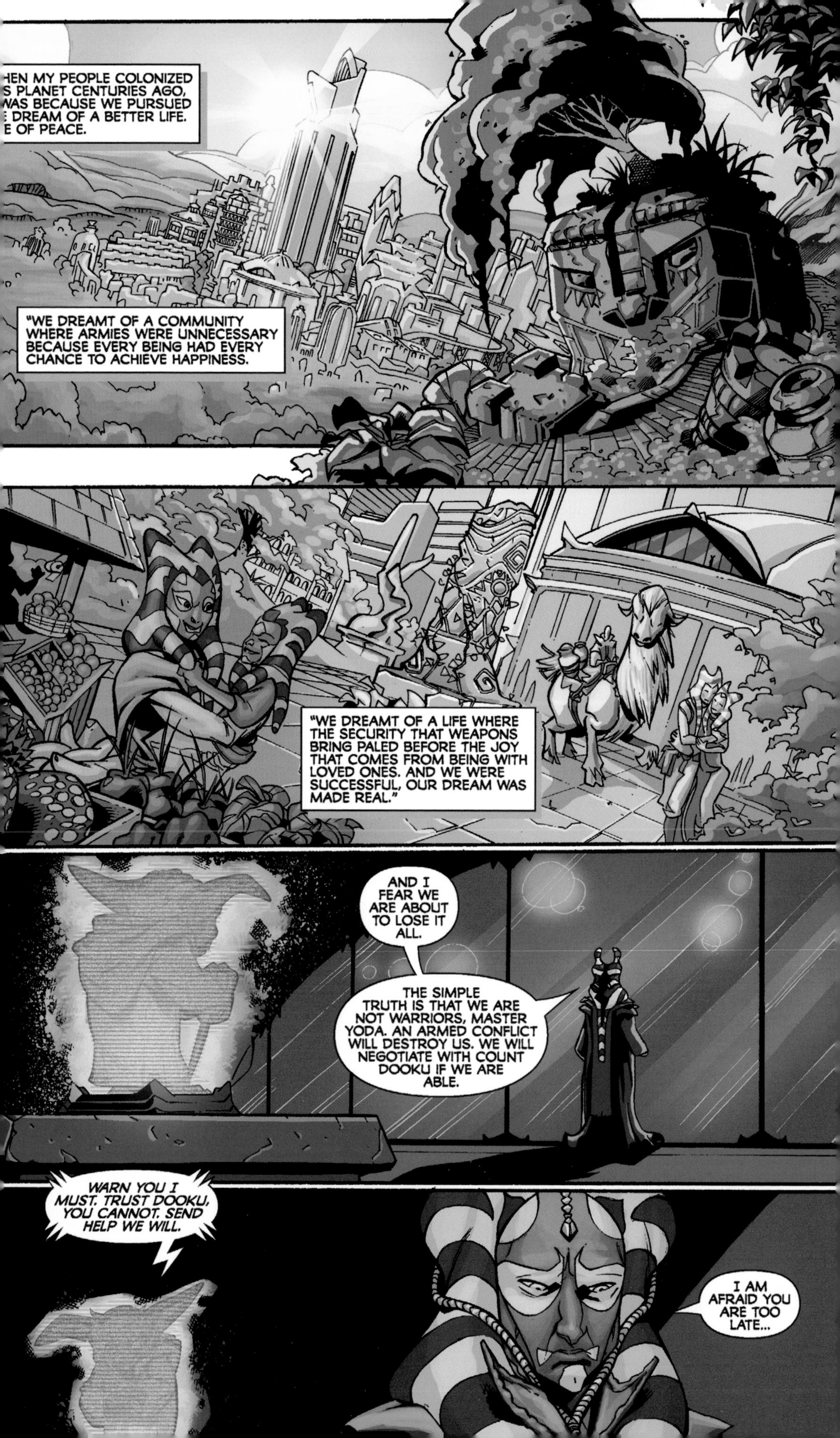
HEN MY PEOPLE COLONIZED
S PLANET CENTURIES AGO,
WAS BECAUSE WE PURSUED
DREAM OF A BETTER LIFE.
E OF PEACE.
"WE DREAMT OF A COMMUNITY WHERE ARMIES WERE UNNECESSARY BECAUSE EVERY BEING HAD EVERY CHANCE TO ACHIEVE HAPPINESS.
"WE DREAMT OF A LIFE WHERE THE SECURITY THAT WEAPONS BRING PALED BEFORE THE JOY THAT COMES FROM BEING WITH LOVED ONES. AND WE WERE SUCCESSFUL, OUR DREAM WAS MADE REAL."
AND I FEAR WE ARE ABOUT TO LOSE IT ALL.
THE SIMPLE TRUTH IS THAT WE ARE NOT WARRIORS, MASTER YODA. AN ARMED CONFLICT WILL DESTROY US. WE WILL NEGOTIATE WITH COUNT DOOKU IF WE ARE ABLE.
WARN YOU I MUST. TRUST DOOKU, YOU CANNOT. SEND HELP WE WILL.
I AM AFRAID YOU ARE TOO LATE...

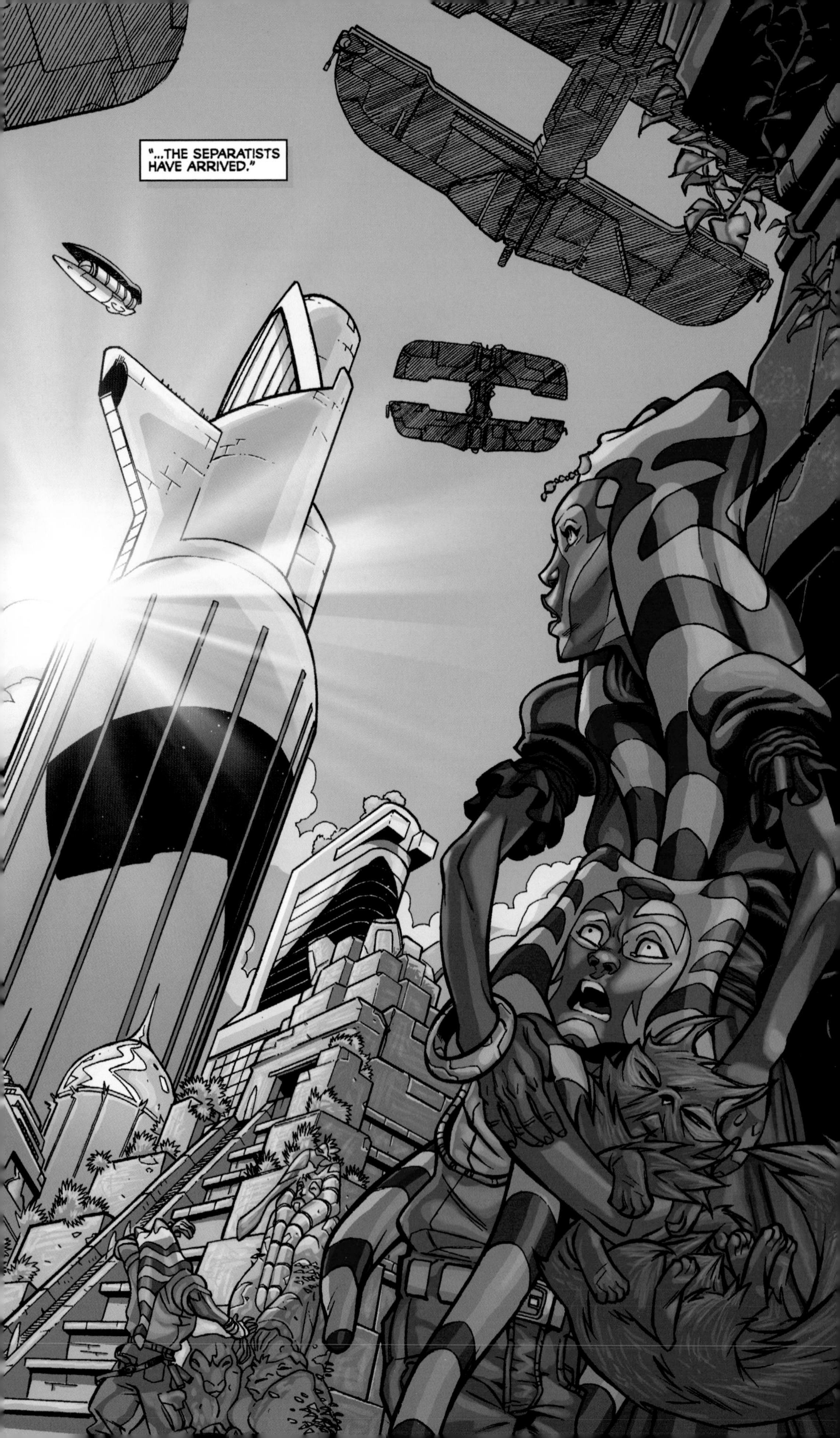
"...THE SEPARATISTS HAVE ARRIVED."

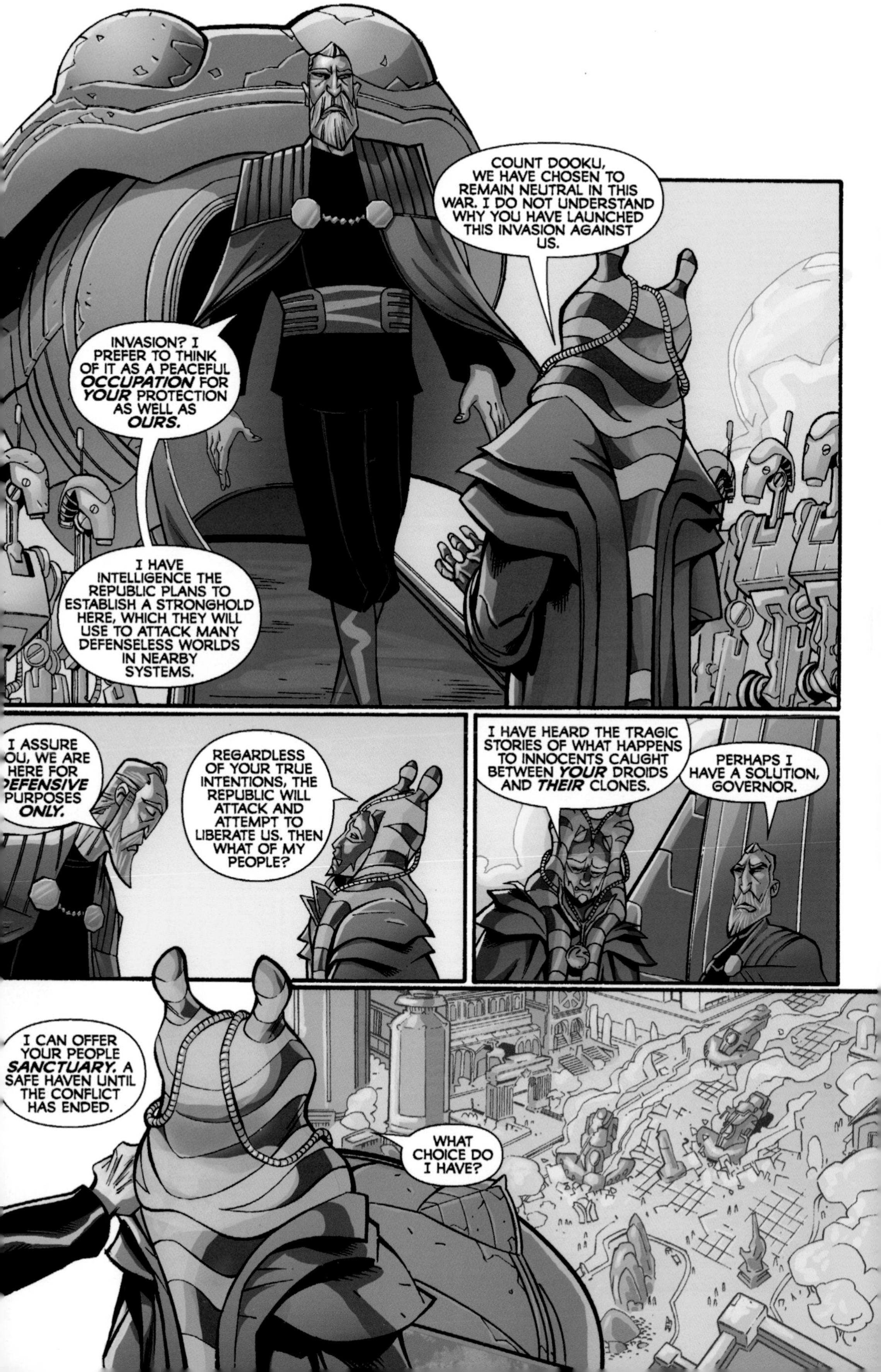
COUNT DOOKU, WE HAVE CHOSEN TO REMAIN NEUTRAL IN THIS WAR. I DO NOT UNDERSTAND WHY YOU HAVE LAUNCHED THIS INVASION AGAINST US.
INVASION? I PREFER TO THINK OF IT AS A PEACEFUL *OCCUPATION* FOR *YOUR* PROTECTION AS WELL AS *OURS.*
I HAVE INTELLIGENCE THE REPUBLIC PLANS TO ESTABLISH A STRONGHOLD HERE, WHICH THEY WILL USE TO ATTACK MANY DEFENSELESS WORLDS IN NEARBY SYSTEMS.
I ASSURE OU, WE ARE HERE FOR EFENSIVE PURPOSES *ONLY.*
REGARDLESS OF YOUR TRUE INTENTIONS, THE REPUBLIC WILL ATTACK AND ATTEMPT TO LIBERATE US. THEN WHAT OF MY PEOPLE?
I HAVE HEARD THE TRAGIC STORIES OF WHAT HAPPENS TO INNOCENTS CAUGHT BETWEEN *YOUR* DROIDS AND *THEIR* CLONES.
PERHAPS I HAVE A SOLUTION, GOVERNOR.
I CAN OFFER YOUR PEOPLE *SANCTUARY.* A SAFE HAVEN UNTIL THE CONFLICT HAS ENDED.
WHAT CHOICE DO I HAVE?

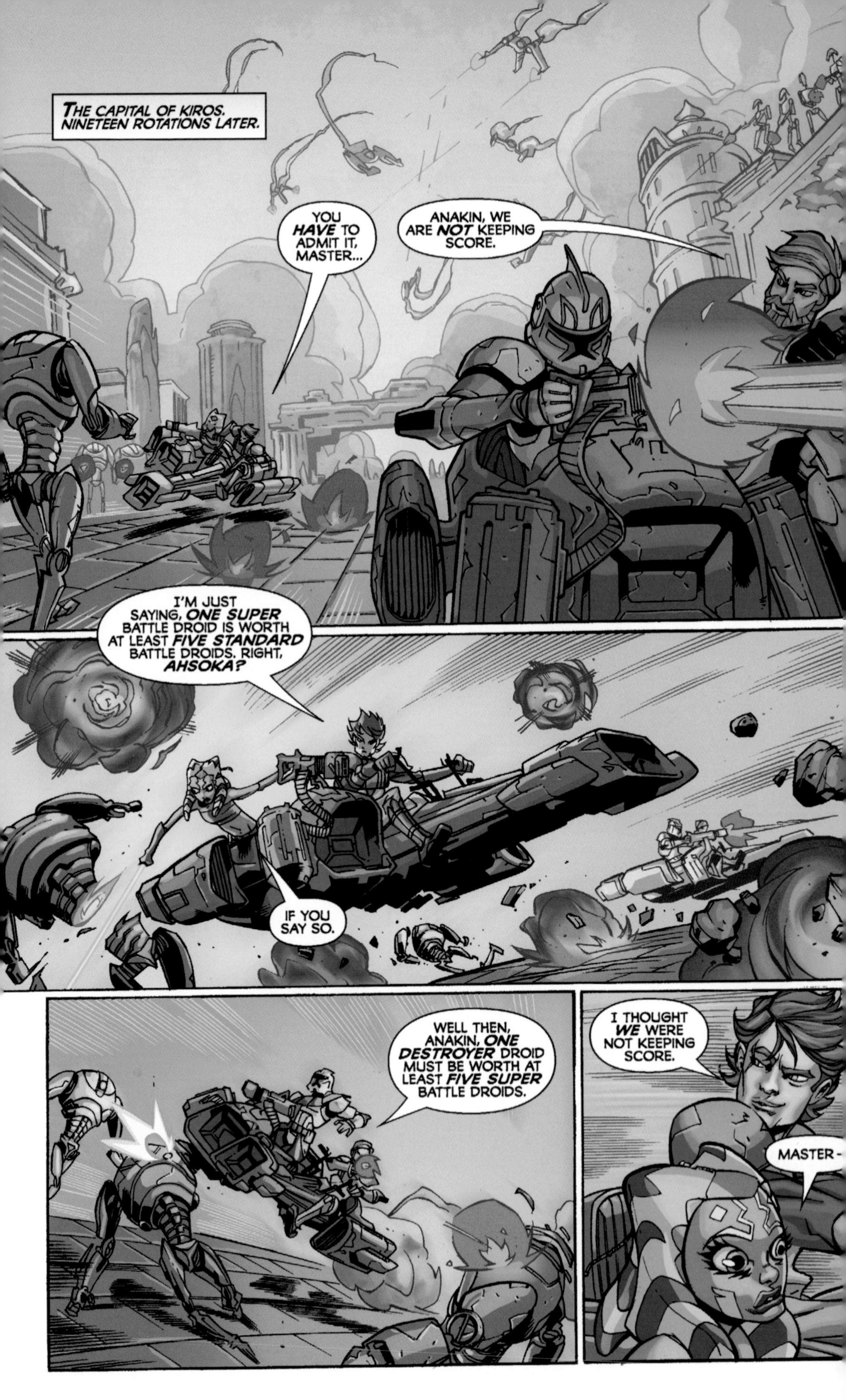
THE CAPITAL OF KIROS. NINETEEN ROTATIONS LATER.
YOU HAVE TO ADMIT IT, MASTER...
ANAKIN, WE ARE NOT KEEPING SCORE.
I'M JUST SAYING, ONE SUPER BATTLE DROID IS WORTH AT LEAST FIVE STANDARD BATTLE DROIDS. RIGHT, AHSOKA?
IF YOU SAY SO.
WELL THEN, ANAKIN, ONE DESTROYER DROID MUST BE WORTH AT LEAST FIVE SUPER BATTLE DROIDS.
I THOUGHT WE WERE NOT KEEPING SCORE.
MASTER -

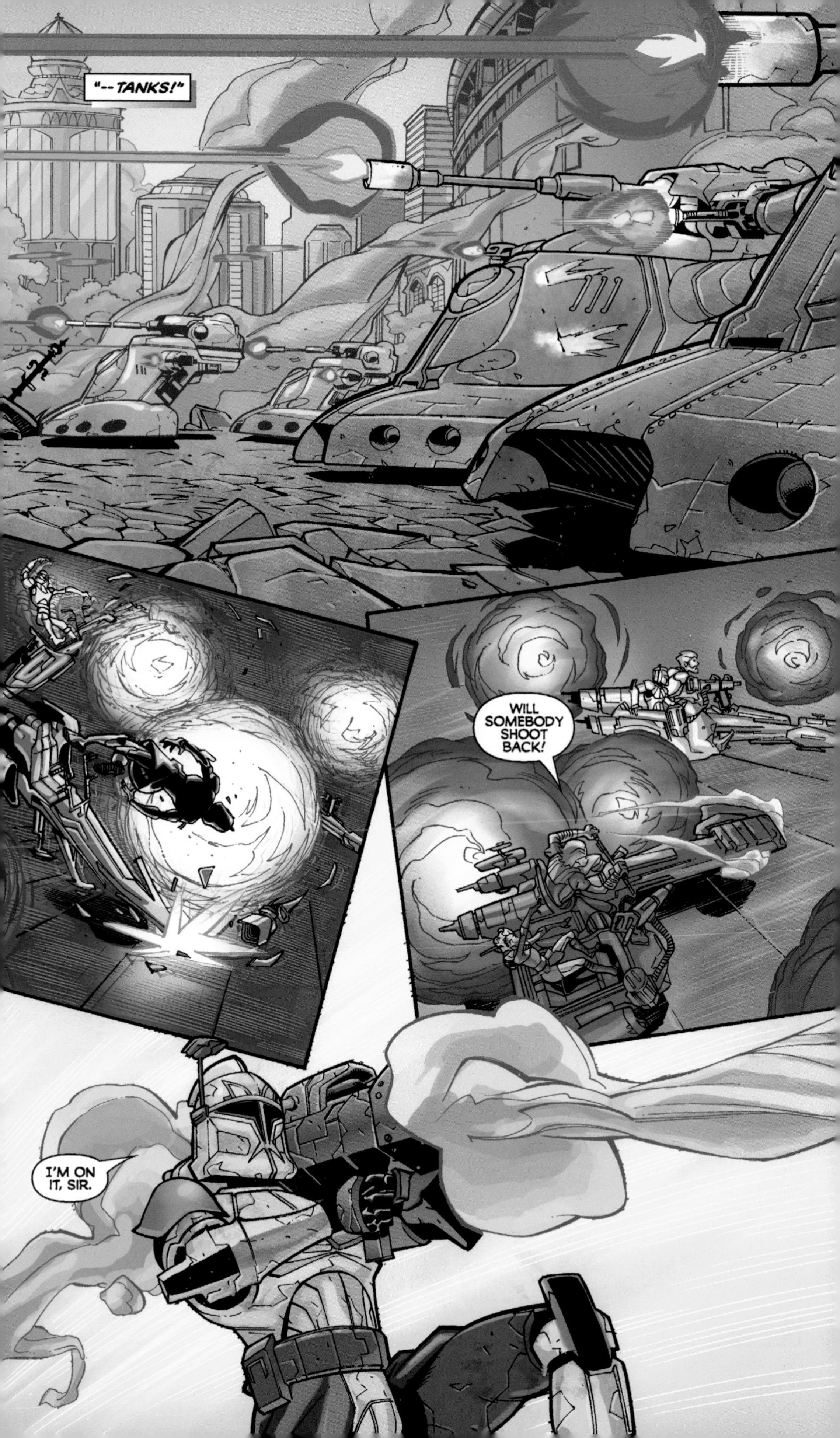
"--TANKS!"
WILL SOMEBODY SHOOT BACK!
I'M ON IT, SIR.

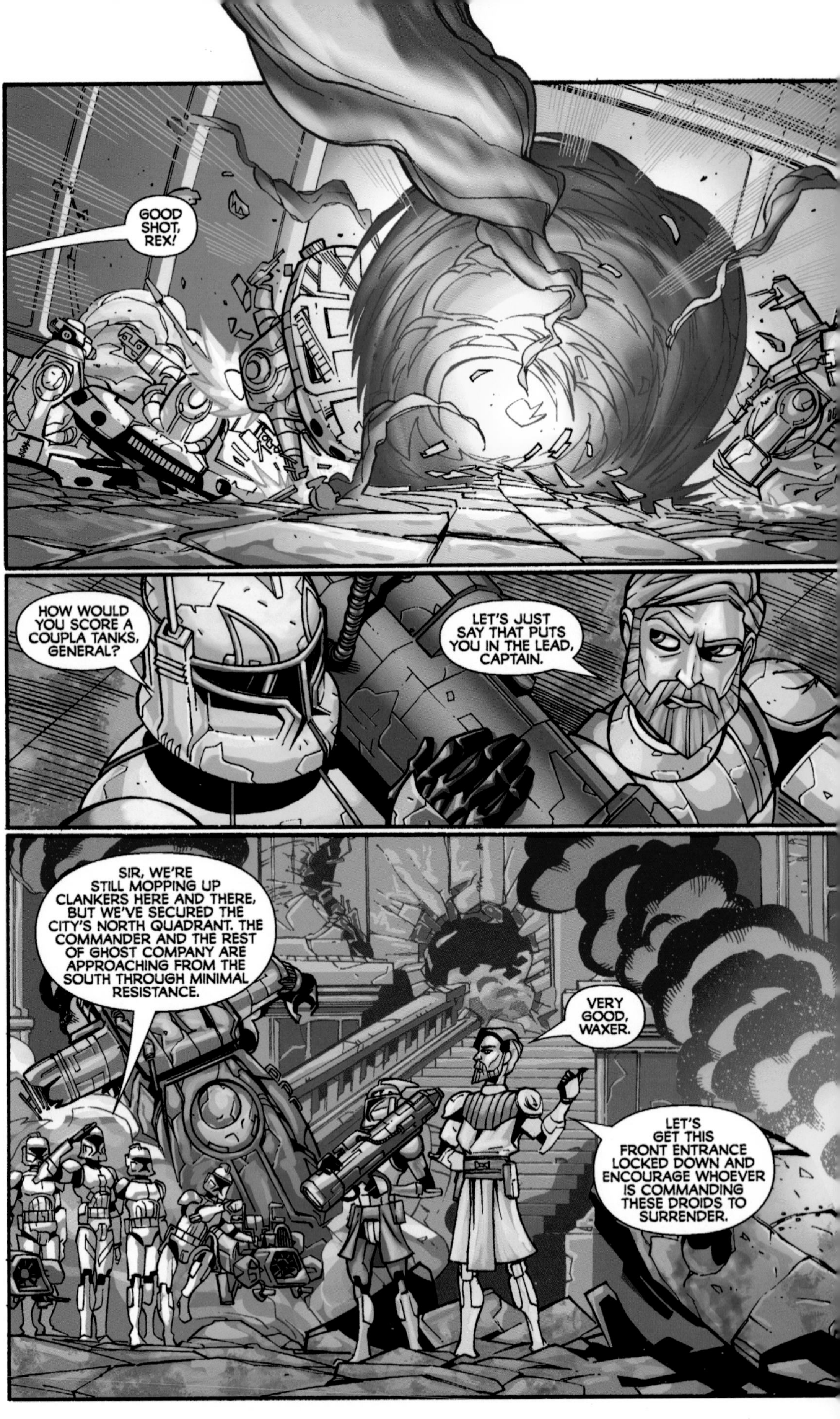
GOOD SHOT, REX!
HOW WOULD YOU SCORE A COUPLA TANKS, GENERAL?
LET'S JUST SAY THAT PUTS YOU IN THE LEAD, CAPTAIN.
SIR, WE'RE STILL MOPPING UP CLANKERS HERE AND THERE, BUT WE'VE SECURED THE CITY'S NORTH QUADRANT. THE COMMANDER AND THE REST OF GHOST COMPANY ARE APPROACHING FROM THE SOUTH THROUGH MINIMAL RESISTANCE.
VERY GOOD, WAXER.
LET'S GET THIS FRONT ENTRANCE LOCKED DOWN AND ENCOURAGE WHOEVER IS COMMANDING THESE DROIDS TO SURRENDER.

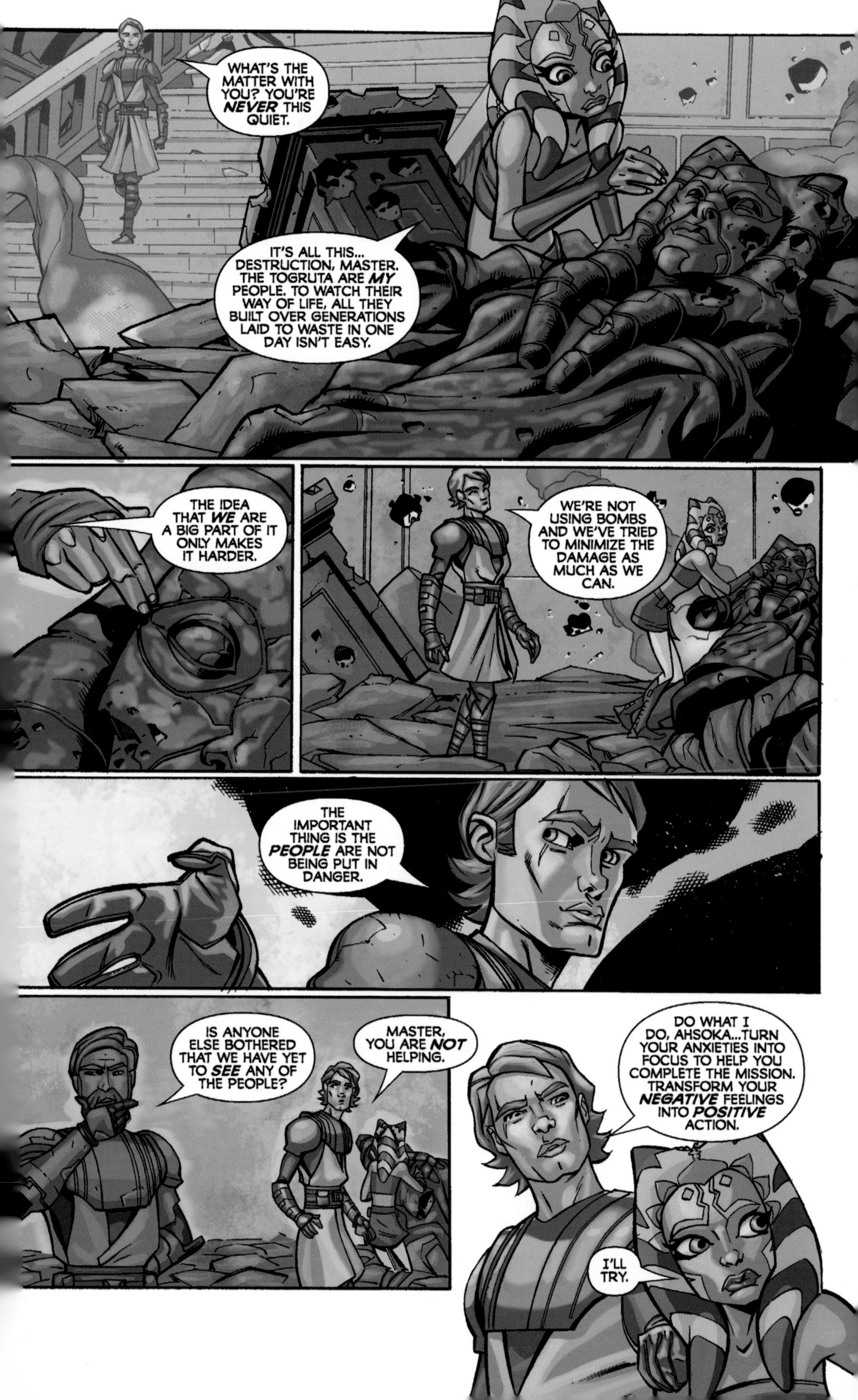
WHAT'S THE MATTER WITH YOU? YOU'RE NEVER THIS QUIET.
IT'S ALL THIS... DESTRUCTION, MASTER. THE TOGRUTA ARE MY PEOPLE. TO WATCH THEIR WAY OF LIFE, ALL THEY BUILT OVER GENERATIONS LAID TO WASTE IN ONE DAY ISN'T EASY.
THE IDEA THAT WE ARE A BIG PART OF IT ONLY MAKES IT HARDER.
WE'RE NOT USING BOMBS AND WE'VE TRIED TO MINIMIZE THE DAMAGE AS MUCH AS WE CAN.
THE IMPORTANT THING IS THE PEOPLE ARE NOT BEING PUT IN DANGER.
IS ANYONE ELSE BOTHERED THAT WE HAVE YET TO SEE ANY OF THE PEOPLE?
MASTER, YOU ARE NOT HELPING.
DO WHAT I DO, AHSOKA...TURN YOUR ANXIETIES INTO FOCUS TO HELP YOU COMPLETE THE MISSION. TRANSFORM YOUR NEGATIVE FEELINGS INTO POSITIVE ACTION.
I'LL TRY.

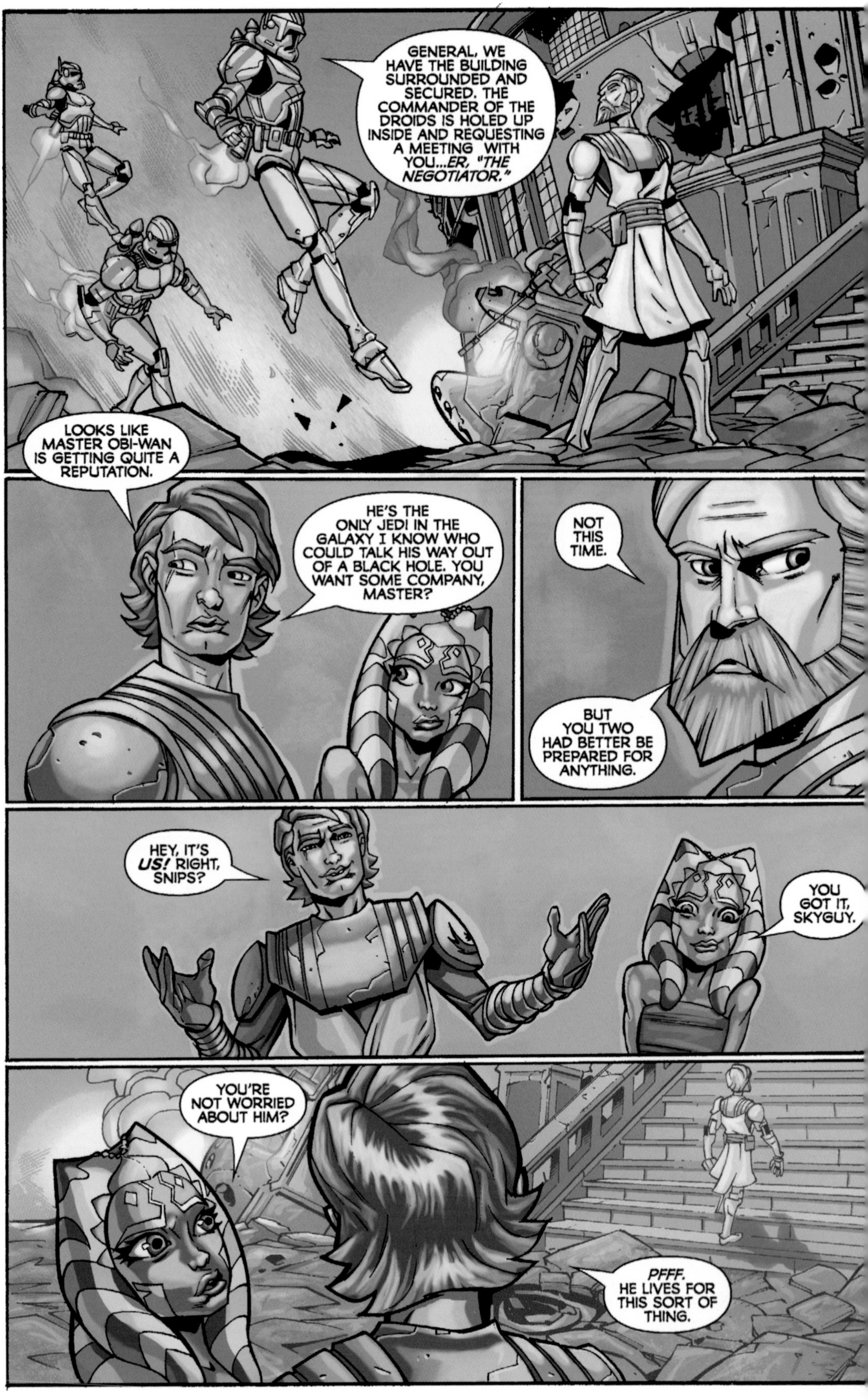
GENERAL, WE HAVE THE BUILDING SURROUNDED AND SECURED. THE COMMANDER OF THE DROIDS IS HOLED UP INSIDE AND REQUESTING A MEETING WITH YOU...*ER, "THE NEGOTIATOR."*
LOOKS LIKE MASTER OBI-WAN IS GETTING QUITE A REPUTATION.
HE'S THE ONLY JEDI IN THE GALAXY I KNOW WHO COULD TALK HIS WAY OUT OF A BLACK HOLE. YOU WANT SOME COMPANY, MASTER?
NOT THIS TIME.
BUT YOU TWO HAD BETTER BE PREPARED FOR ANYTHING.
HEY, IT'S *US!* RIGHT, SNIPS?
YOU GOT IT, SKYGUY.
YOU'RE NOT WORRIED ABOUT HIM?
PFFF. HE LIVES FOR THIS SORT OF THING.

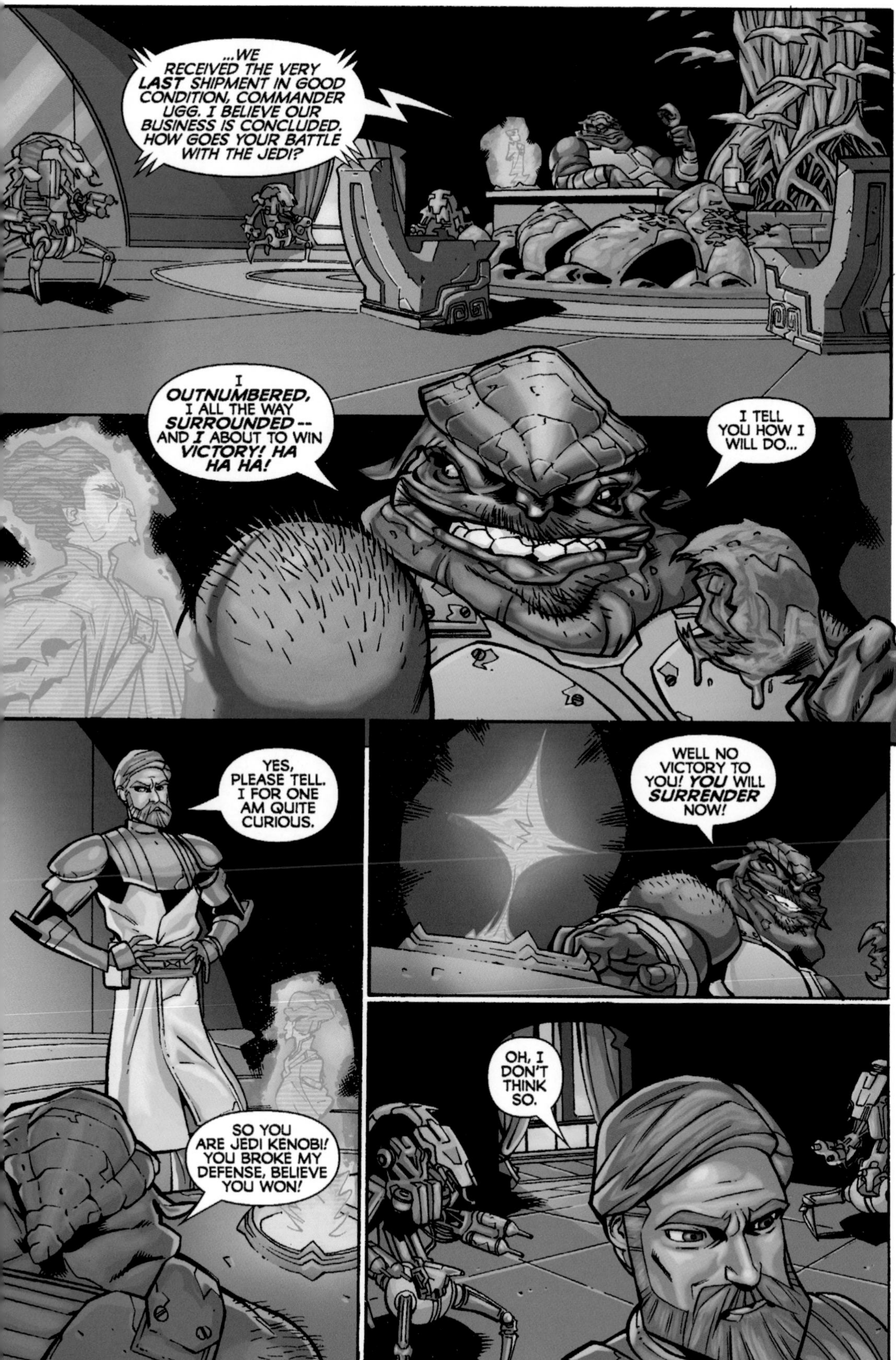
...WE RECEIVED THE VERY LAST SHIPMENT IN GOOD CONDITION, COMMANDER UGG. I BELIEVE OUR BUSINESS IS CONCLUDED. HOW GOES YOUR BATTLE WITH THE JEDI?
I OUTNUMBERED, I ALL THE WAY SURROUNDED-- AND I ABOUT TO WIN VICTORY! HA HA HA!
I TELL YOU HOW I WILL DO...
YES, PLEASE TELL. I FOR ONE AM QUITE CURIOUS.
SO YOU ARE JEDI KENOBI! YOU BROKE MY DEFENSE, BELIEVE YOU WON!
WELL NO VICTORY TO YOU! YOU WILL SURRENDER NOW!
OH, I DON'T THINK SO.

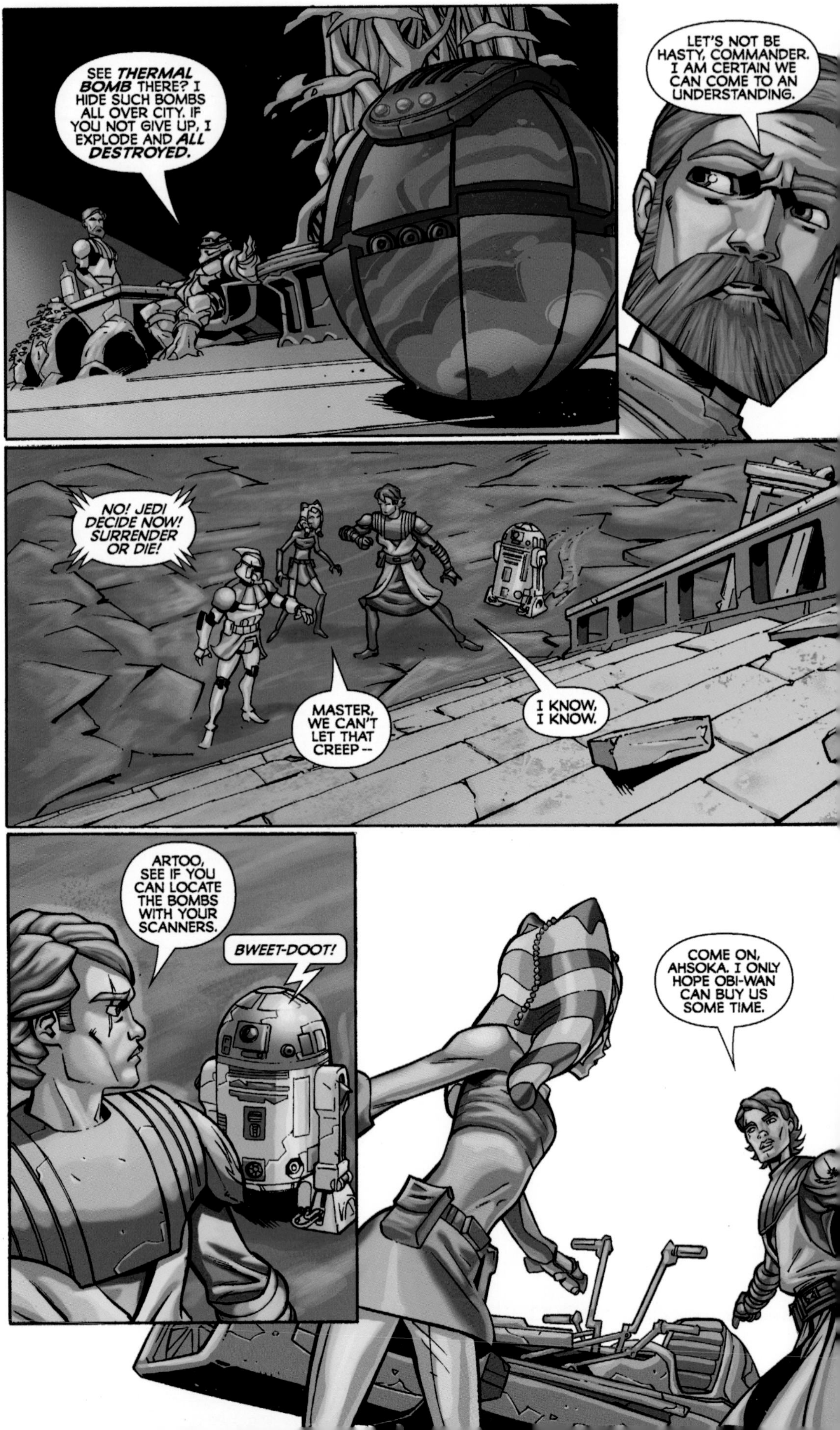
SEE *THERMAL BOMB* THERE? I HIDE SUCH BOMBS ALL OVER CITY. IF YOU NOT GIVE UP, I EXPLODE AND *ALL DESTROYED*.
LET'S NOT BE HASTY, COMMANDER. I AM CERTAIN WE CAN COME TO AN UNDERSTANDING.
NO! JEDI DECIDE NOW! SURRENDER OR DIE!
MASTER, WE CAN'T LET THAT CREEP --
I KNOW, I KNOW.
ARTOO, SEE IF YOU CAN LOCATE THE BOMBS WITH YOUR SCANNERS.
BWEET-DOOT!
COME ON, AHSOKA. I ONLY HOPE OBI-WAN CAN BUY US SOME TIME.

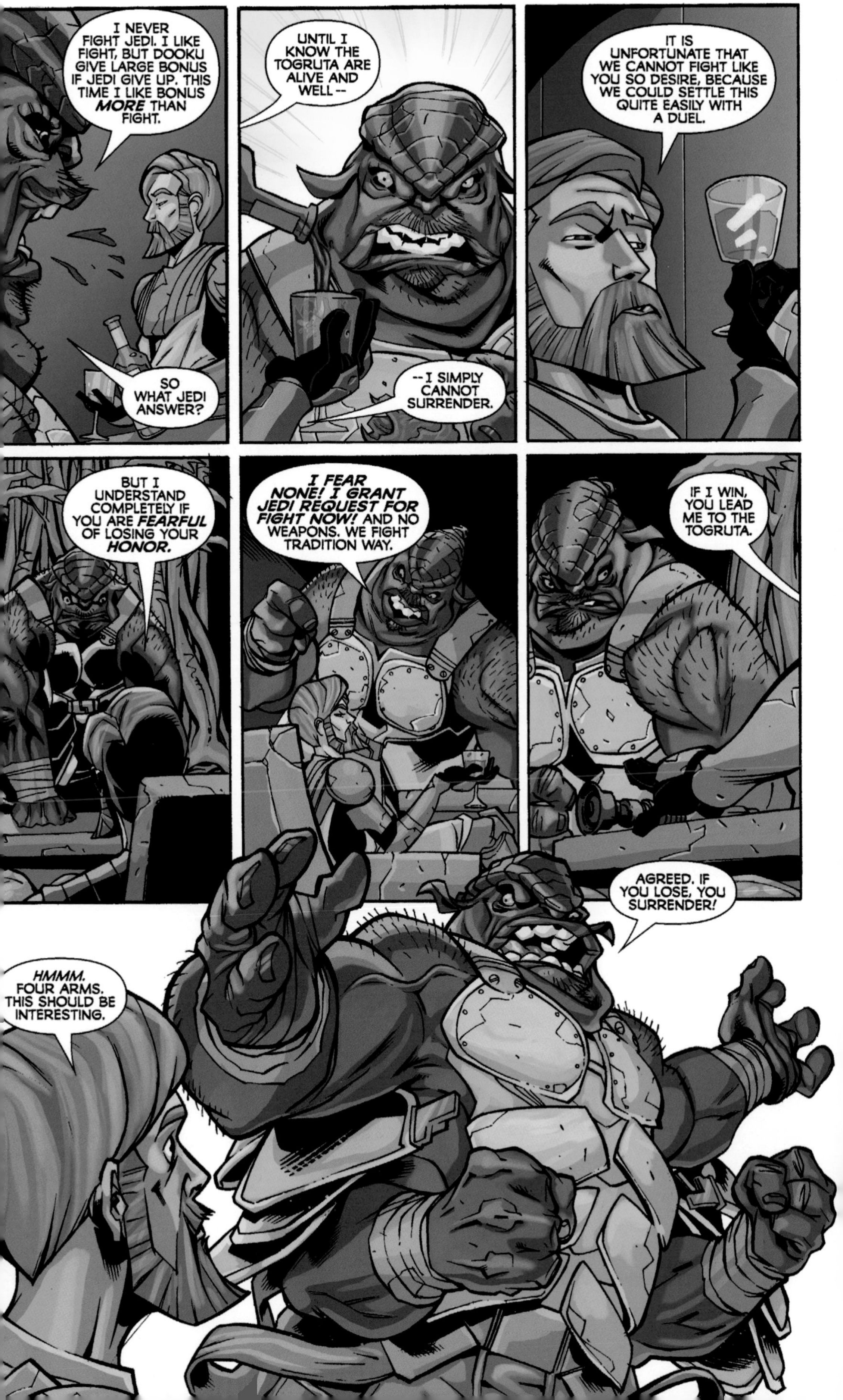

I NEVER FIGHT JEDI. I LIKE FIGHT, BUT DOOKU GIVE LARGE BONUS IF JEDI GIVE UP. THIS TIME I LIKE BONUS *MORE* THAN FIGHT.
SO WHAT JEDI ANSWER?
UNTIL I KNOW THE TOGRUTA ARE ALIVE AND WELL --
-- I SIMPLY CANNOT SURRENDER.
IT IS UNFORTUNATE THAT WE CANNOT FIGHT LIKE YOU SO DESIRE, BECAUSE WE COULD SETTLE THIS QUITE EASILY WITH A DUEL.
BUT I UNDERSTAND COMPLETELY IF YOU ARE *FEARFUL* OF LOSING YOUR *HONOR.*
I FEAR NONE! I GRANT JEDI REQUEST FOR FIGHT NOW! AND NO WEAPONS. WE FIGHT TRADITION WAY.
IF I WIN, YOU LEAD ME TO THE TOGRUTA.
AGREED. IF YOU LOSE, YOU SURRENDER!
HMMM. FOUR ARMS. THIS SHOULD BE INTERESTING.

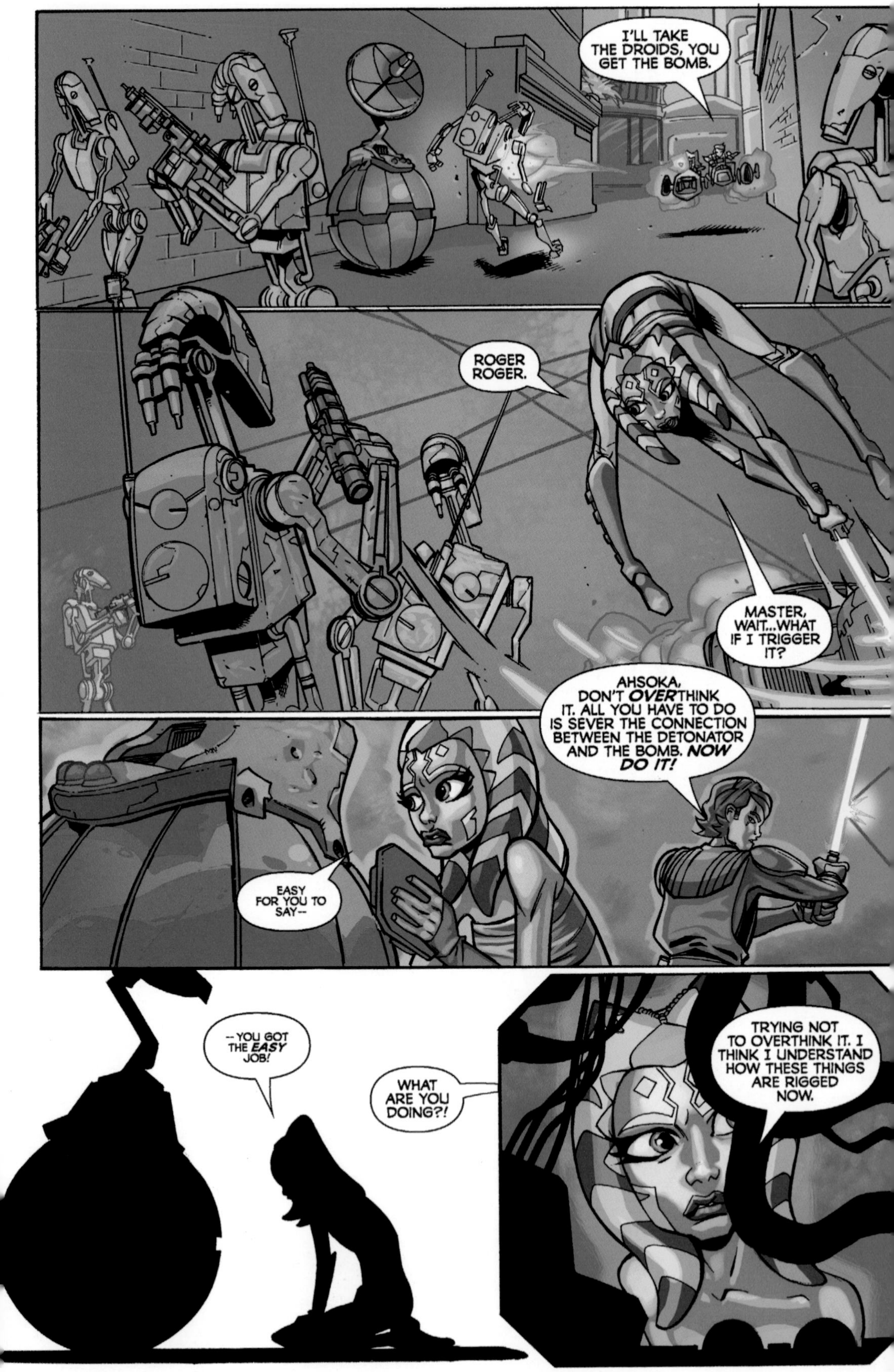
I'LL TAKE THE DROIDS, YOU GET THE BOMB.
ROGER ROGER.
MASTER, WAIT...WHAT IF I TRIGGER IT?
AHSOKA, DON'T *OVER*THINK IT. ALL YOU HAVE TO DO IS SEVER THE CONNECTION BETWEEN THE DETONATOR AND THE BOMB. *NOW DO IT!*
EASY FOR YOU TO SAY--
--YOU GOT THE *EASY* JOB!
WHAT ARE YOU DOING?!
TRYING NOT TO OVERTHINK IT. I THINK I UNDERSTAND HOW THESE THINGS ARE RIGGED NOW.

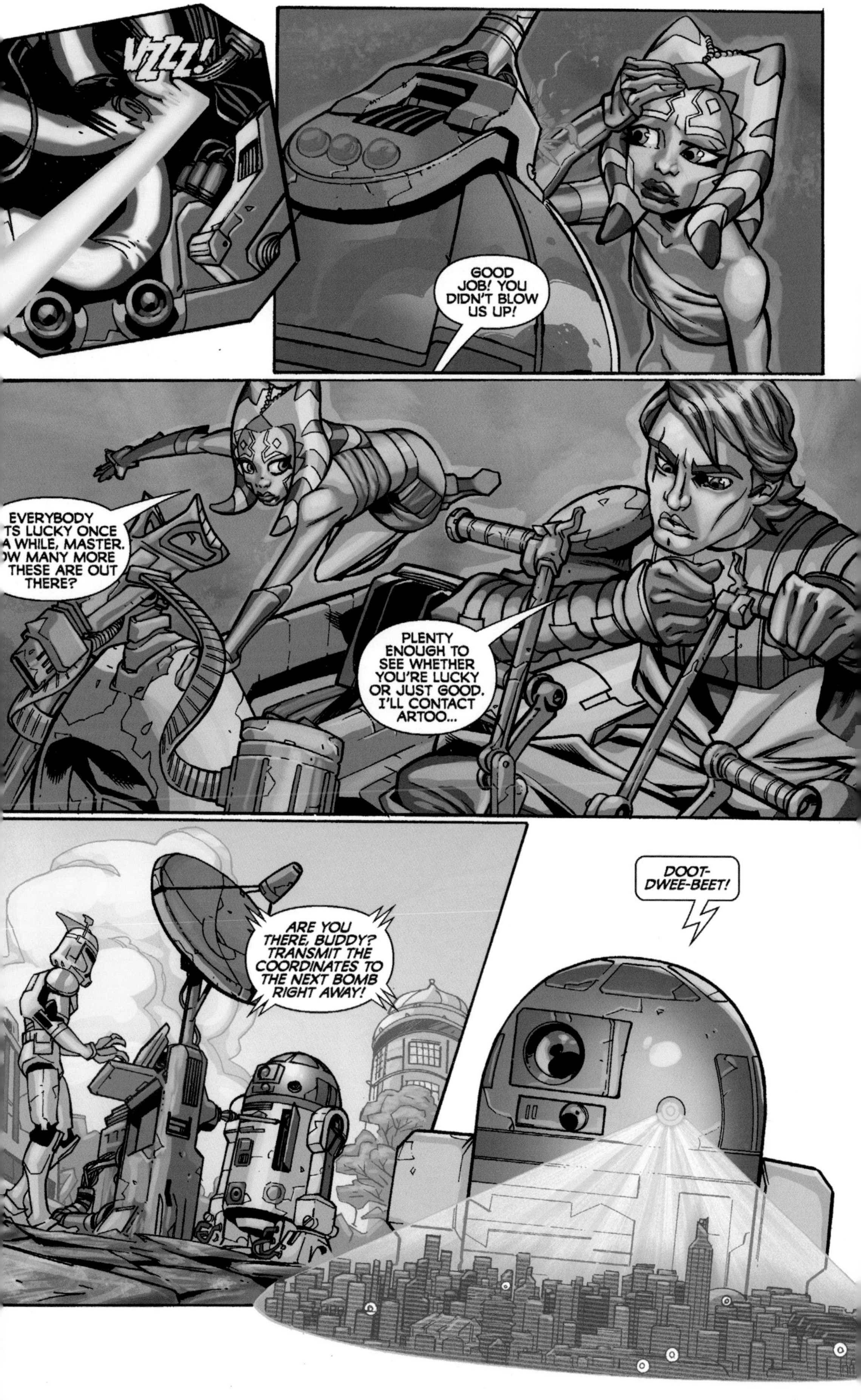
VZZZ!
GOOD JOB! YOU DIDN'T BLOW US UP!
EVERYBODY TS LUCKY ONCE A WHILE, MASTER. OW MANY MORE THESE ARE OUT THERE?
PLENTY ENOUGH TO SEE WHETHER YOU'RE LUCKY OR JUST GOOD. I'LL CONTACT ARTOO...
ARE YOU THERE, BUDDY? TRANSMIT THE COORDINATES TO THE NEXT BOMB RIGHT AWAY!
DOOT-DWEE-BEET!

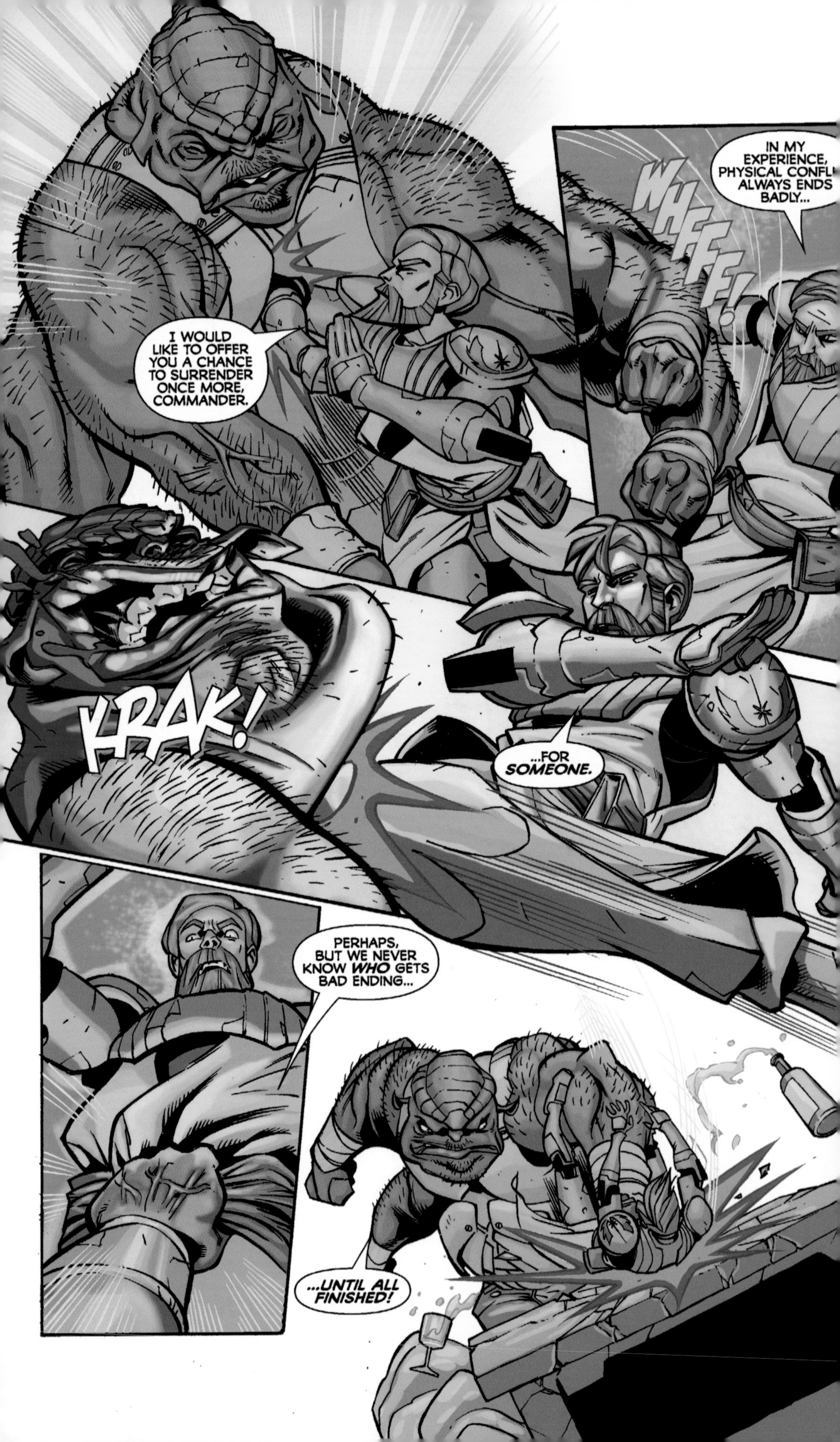
I WOULD LIKE TO OFFER YOU A CHANCE TO SURRENDER ONCE MORE, COMMANDER.
WHFFF!
IN MY EXPERIENCE, PHYSICAL CONFL ALWAYS ENDS BADLY...
KRAK!
...FOR *SOMEONE.*
PERHAPS, BUT WE NEVER KNOW *WHO* GETS BAD ENDING...
...UNTIL ALL FINISHED!

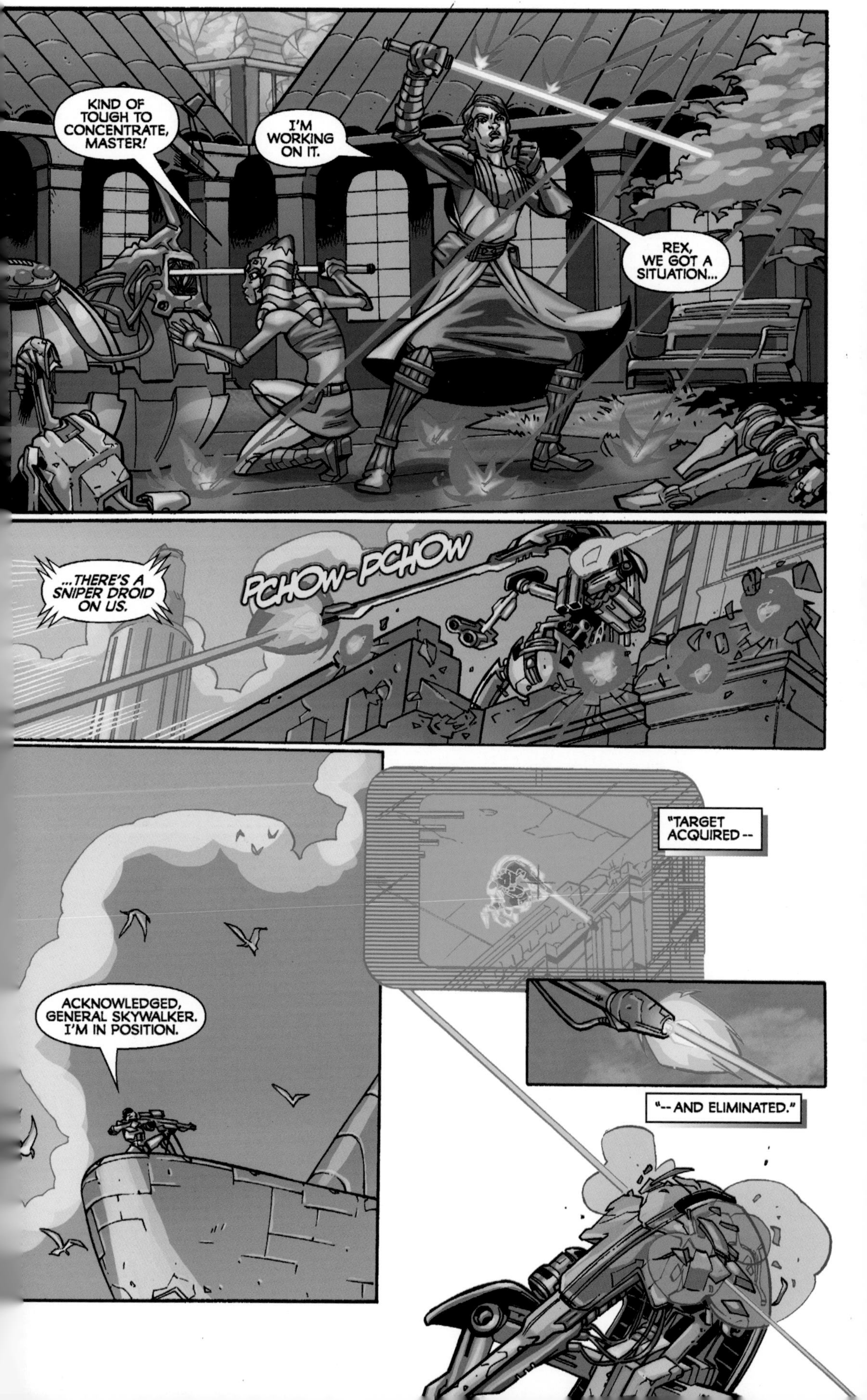
KIND OF TOUGH TO CONCENTRATE, MASTER!
I'M WORKING ON IT.
REX, WE GOT A SITUATION...
...THERE'S A SNIPER DROID ON US.
PCHOW-PCHOW
ACKNOWLEDGED, GENERAL SKYWALKER. I'M IN POSITION.
"TARGET ACQUIRED --
"-- AND ELIMINATED."

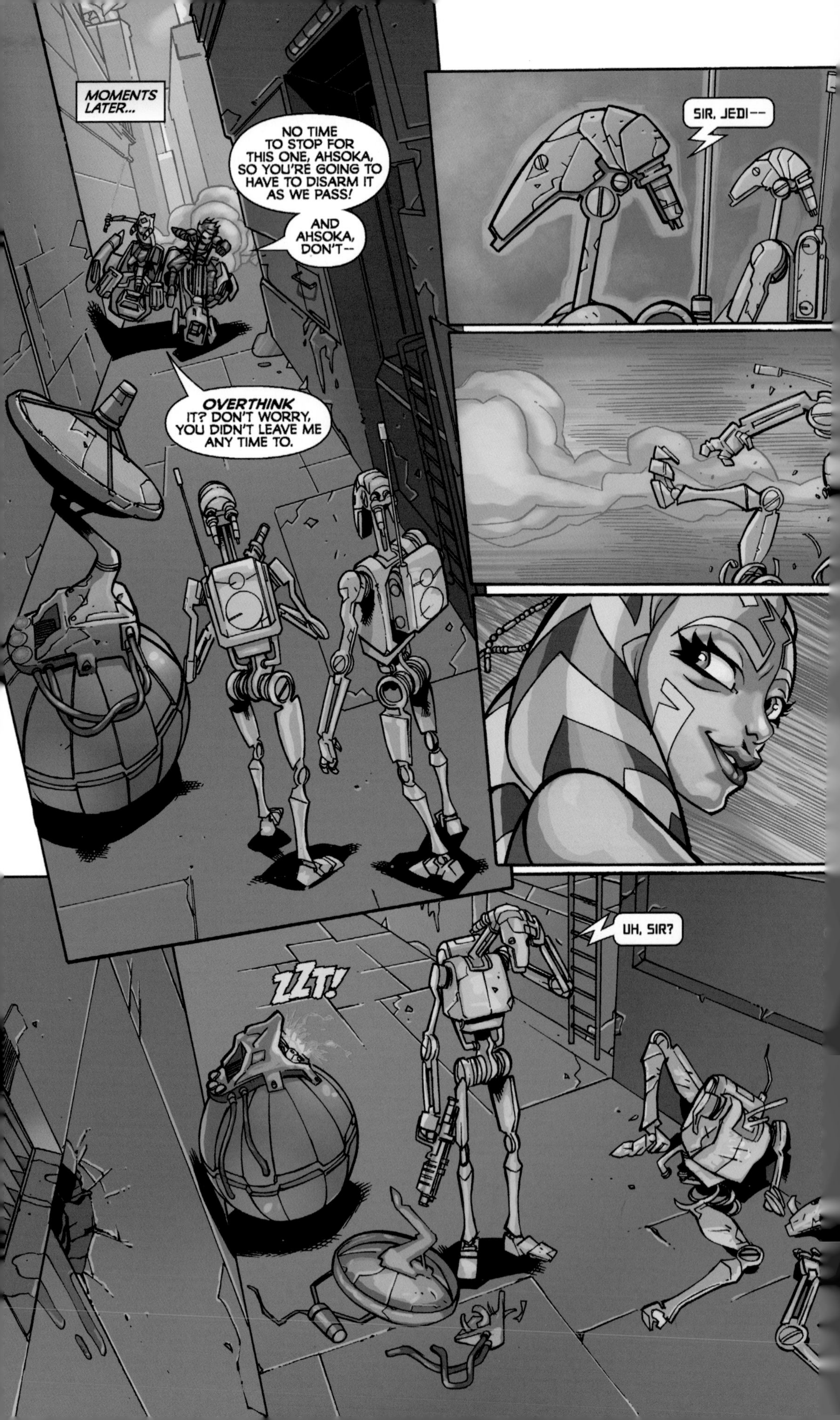
MOMENTS LATER...
NO TIME TO STOP FOR THIS ONE, AHSOKA, SO YOU'RE GOING TO HAVE TO DISARM IT AS WE PASS!
AND AHSOKA, DON'T--
OVERTHINK IT? DON'T WORRY, YOU DIDN'T LEAVE ME ANY TIME TO.
SIR, JEDI--
UH, SIR?
ZZT!

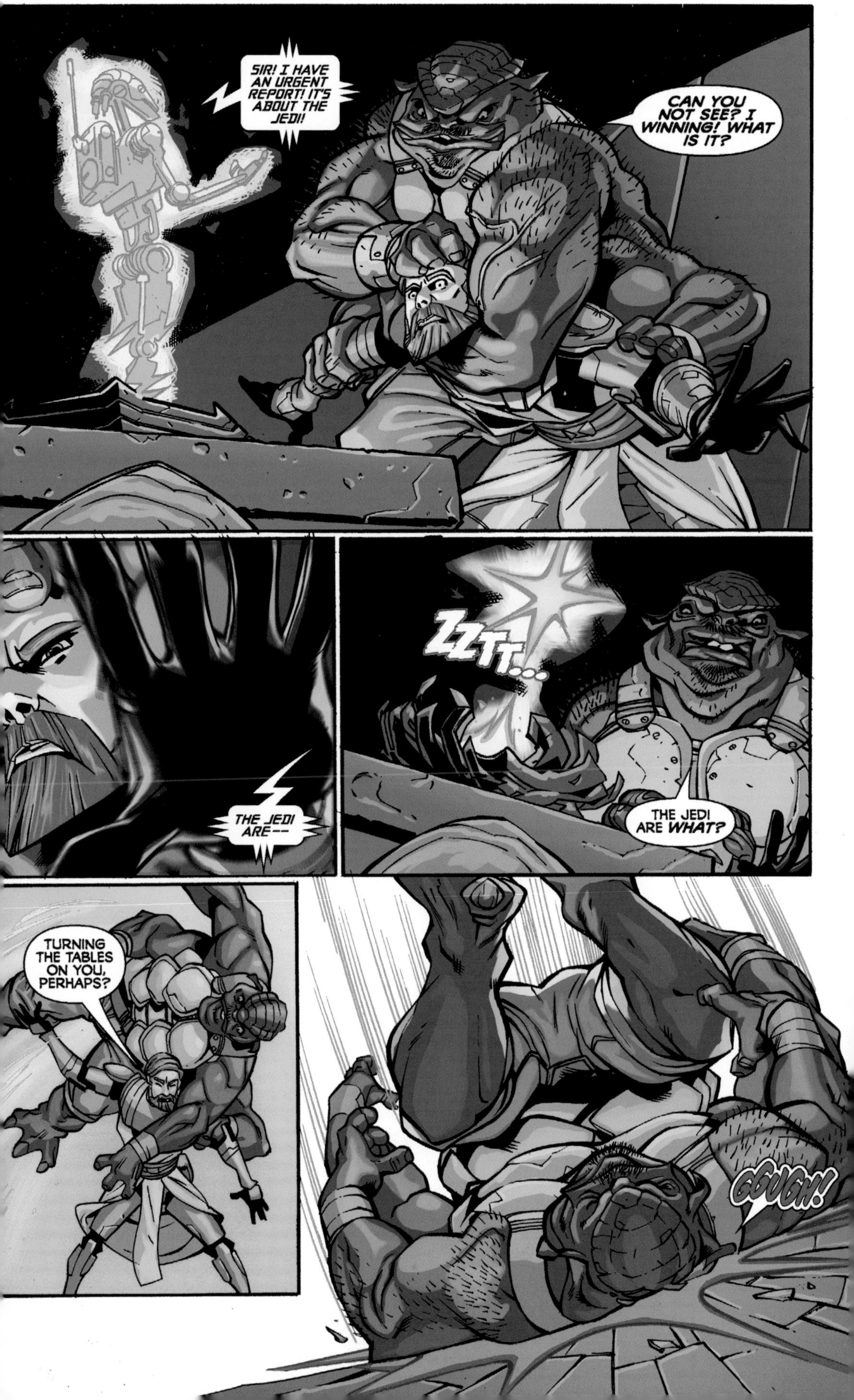
SIR! I HAVE AN URGENT REPORT! IT'S ABOUT THE JEDI!
CAN YOU NOT SEE? I WINNING! WHAT IS IT?
THE JEDI ARE--
ZZTT...
THE JEDI ARE WHAT?
TURNING THE TABLES ON YOU, PERHAPS?
GGUGH!

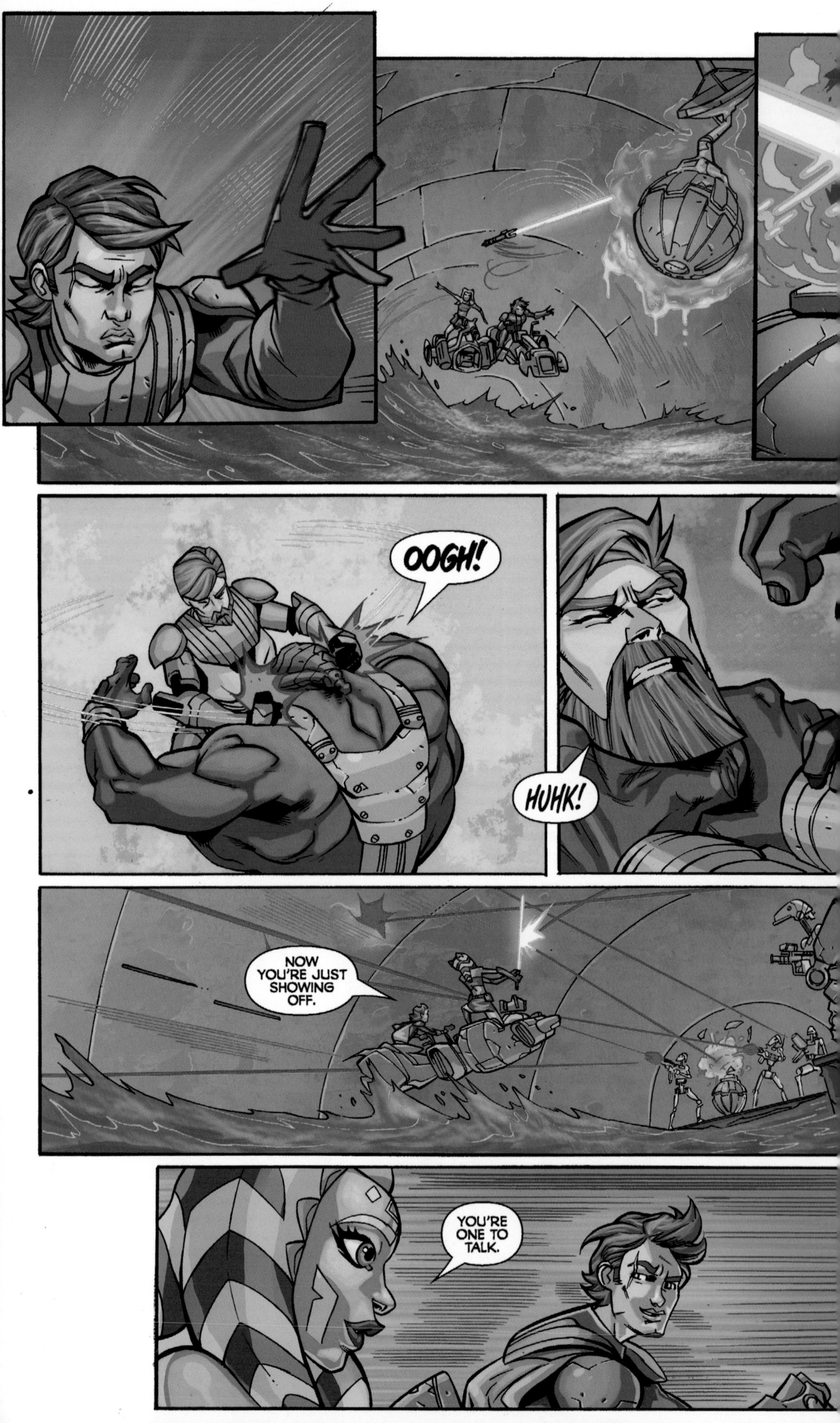
OOGH!
HUHK!
NOW YOU'RE JUST SHOWING OFF.
YOU'RE ONE TO TALK.

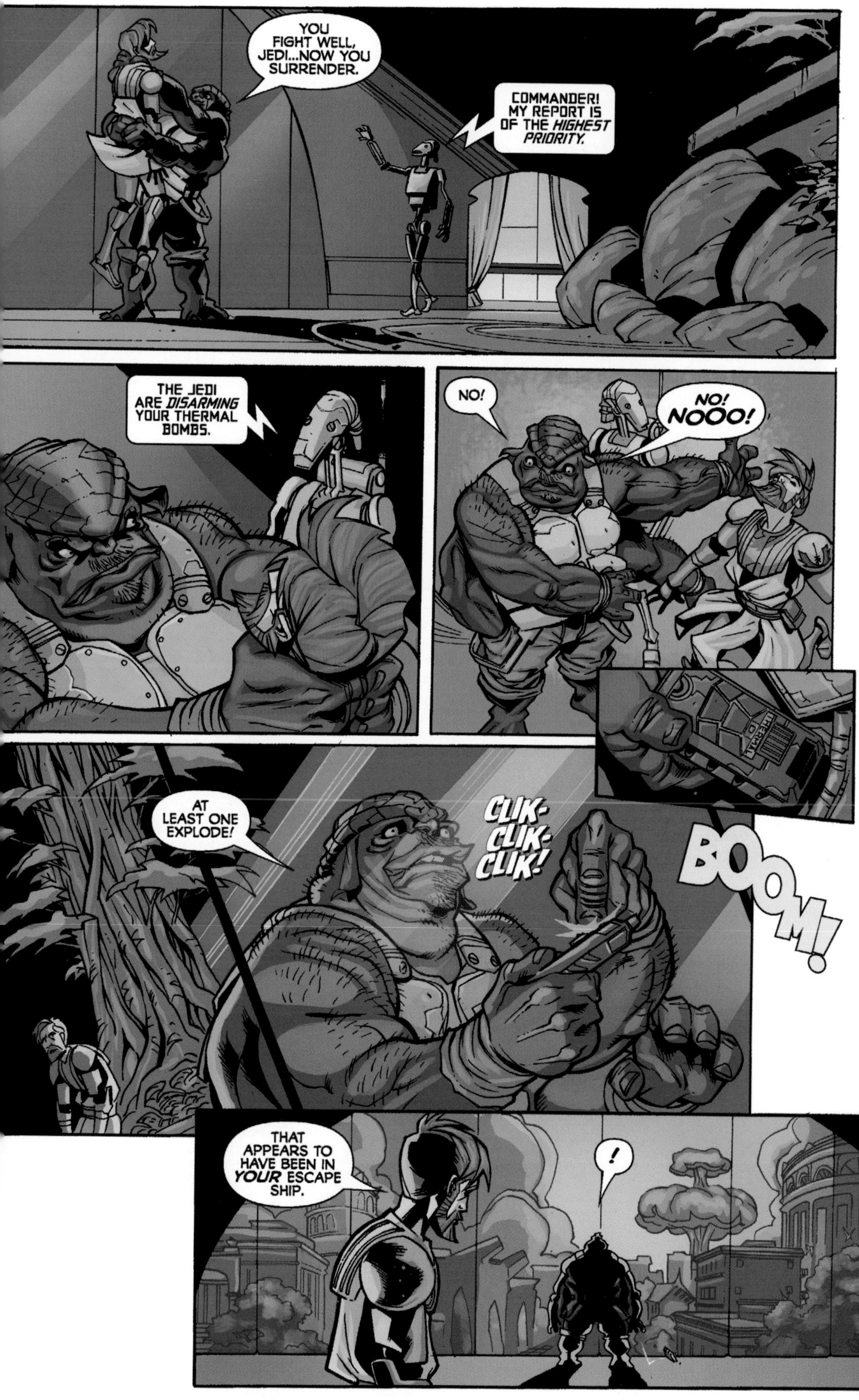
YOU FIGHT WELL, JEDI...NOW YOU SURRENDER.
COMMANDER! MY REPORT IS OF THE *HIGHEST PRIORITY.*
THE JEDI ARE *DISARMING* YOUR THERMAL BOMBS.
NO!
NO! NOOO!
THERMAL D
AT LEAST ONE EXPLODE!
CLIK-CLIK-CLIK!
BOOM!
THAT APPEARS TO HAVE BEEN IN *YOUR* ESCAPE SHIP.
!

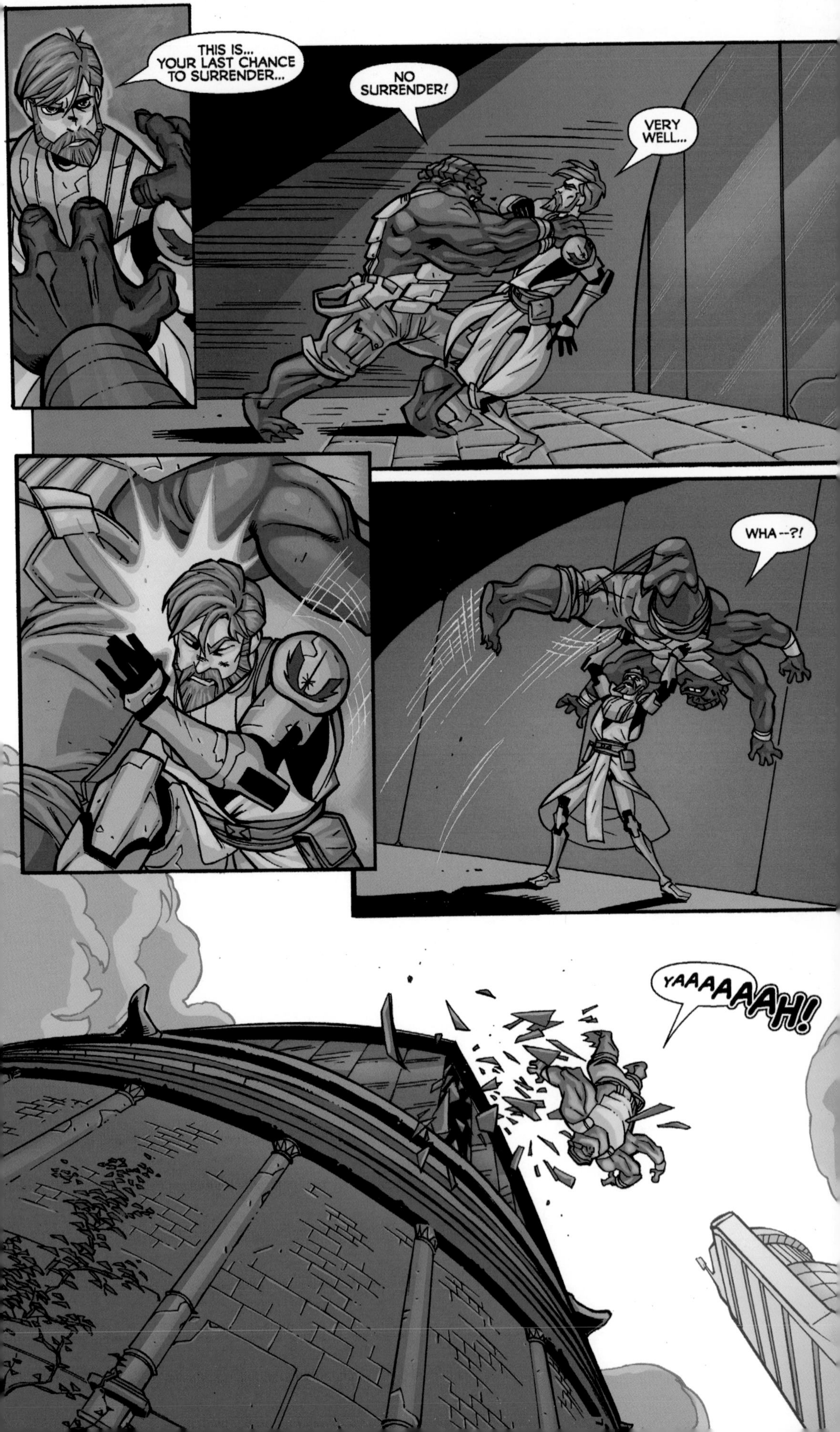
THIS IS... YOUR LAST CHANCE TO SURRENDER...
NO SURRENDER!
VERY WELL...
WHA--?!
YAAAAAAH!

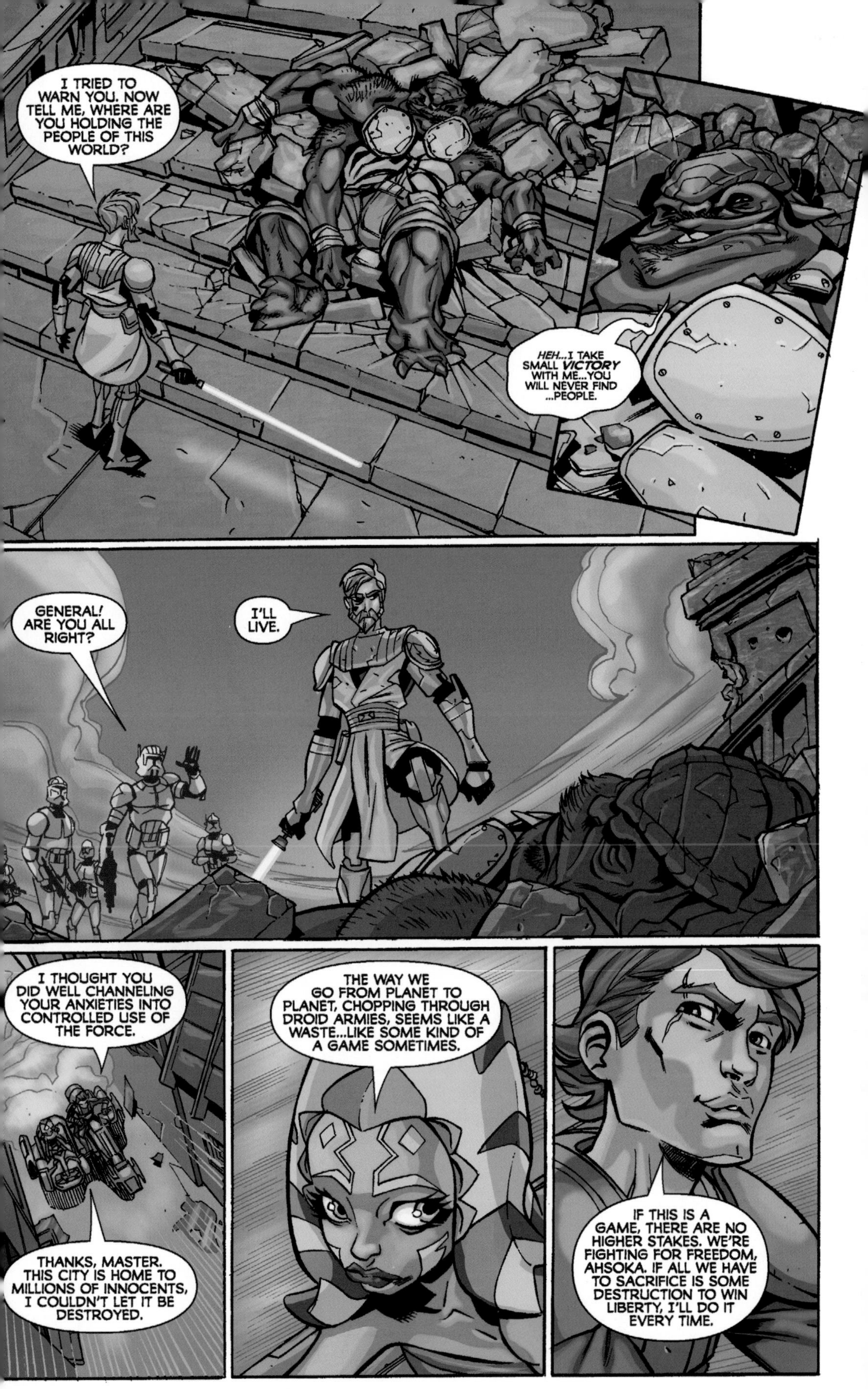
I TRIED TO WARN YOU. NOW TELL ME, WHERE ARE YOU HOLDING THE PEOPLE OF THIS WORLD?
HEH...I TAKE SMALL VICTORY WITH ME...YOU WILL NEVER FIND ...PEOPLE.
GENERAL! ARE YOU ALL RIGHT?
I'LL LIVE.
I THOUGHT YOU DID WELL CHANNELING YOUR ANXIETIES INTO CONTROLLED USE OF THE FORCE.
THANKS, MASTER. THIS CITY IS HOME TO MILLIONS OF INNOCENTS, I COULDN'T LET IT BE DESTROYED.
THE WAY WE GO FROM PLANET TO PLANET, CHOPPING THROUGH DROID ARMIES, SEEMS LIKE A WASTE...LIKE SOME KIND OF A GAME SOMETIMES.
IF THIS IS A GAME, THERE ARE NO HIGHER STAKES. WE'RE FIGHTING FOR FREEDOM, AHSOKA. IF ALL WE HAVE TO SACRIFICE IS SOME DESTRUCTION TO WIN LIBERTY, I'LL DO IT EVERY TIME.

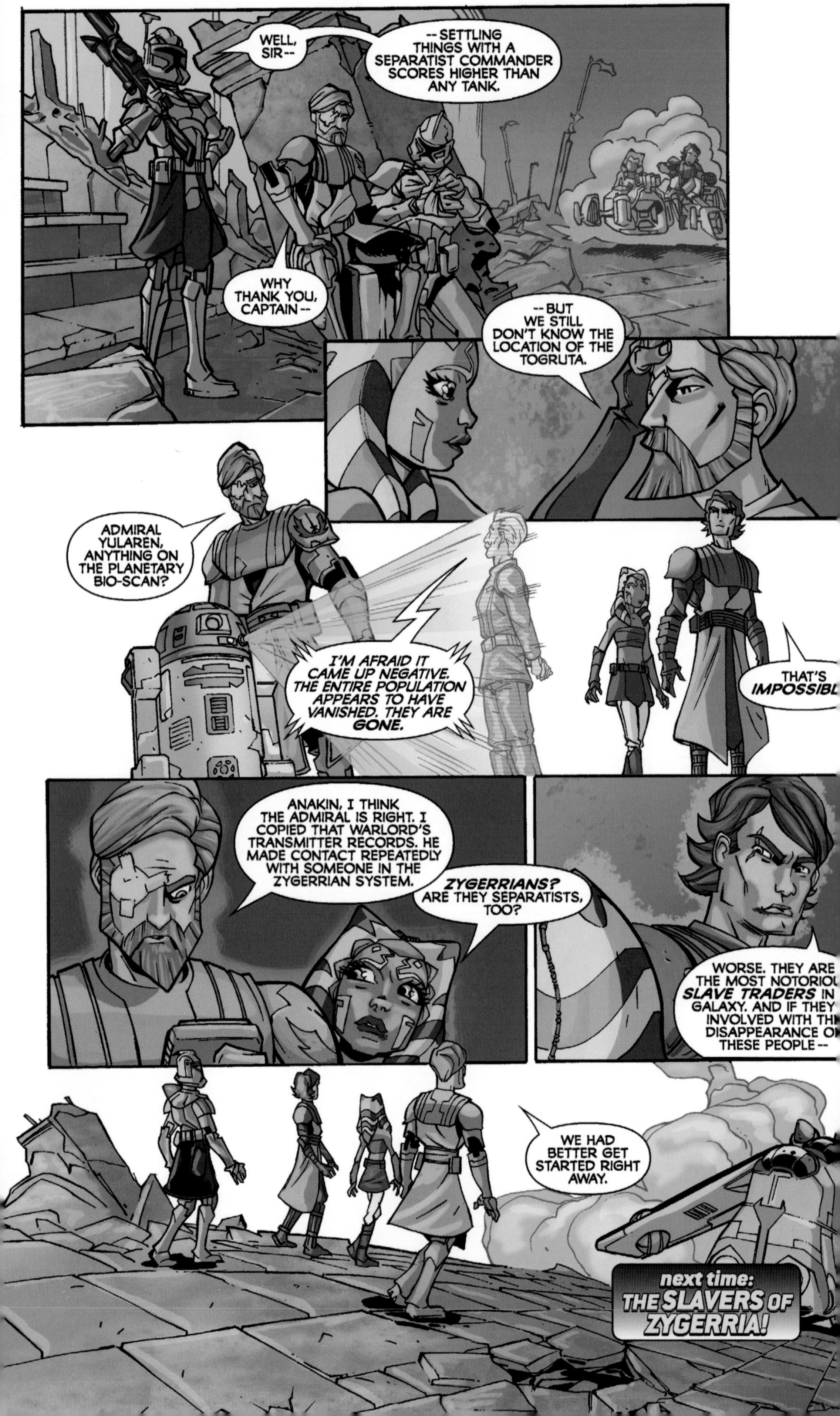
WELL, SIR--
--SETTLING THINGS WITH A SEPARATIST COMMANDER SCORES HIGHER THAN ANY TANK.
WHY THANK YOU, CAPTAIN--
--BUT WE STILL DON'T KNOW THE LOCATION OF THE TOGRUTA.
ADMIRAL YULAREN, ANYTHING ON THE PLANETARY BIO-SCAN?
I'M AFRAID IT CAME UP NEGATIVE. THE ENTIRE POPULATION APPEARS TO HAVE VANISHED. THEY ARE GONE.
THAT'S IMPOSSIBL
ANAKIN, I THINK THE ADMIRAL IS RIGHT. I COPIED THAT WARLORD'S TRANSMITTER RECORDS. HE MADE CONTACT REPEATEDLY WITH SOMEONE IN THE ZYGERRIAN SYSTEM.
ZYGERRIANS? ARE THEY SEPARATISTS, TOO?
WORSE. THEY ARE THE MOST NOTORIOU SLAVE TRADERS IN GALAXY. AND IF THEY INVOLVED WITH TH DISAPPEARANCE O THESE PEOPLE--
WE HAD BETTER GET STARTED RIGHT AWAY.
next time: THE SLAVERS OF ZYGERRIA!